This book belongs to:

- -

For Maddie Doodles, who gave me the inspiration for this book
and made me all that tea while I did it!
Thank you.
K.S.

*Sir Charlie Stinky Socks would like to donate 10% of the royalties from
the sale of this book to Naomi House Children's Hospice.*

EGMONT

We bring stories to life

First published in Great Britain 2008
by Egmont UK Limited
This edition published 2015
The Yellow Building, 1 Nicholas Road
London W11 4AN

www.egmont.co.uk

Text and illustrations copyright © Kristina Stephenson 2008
All rights reserved
Kristina Stephenson has asserted her moral rights

ISBN (PB) 978 1 4052 7769 3

A CIP catalogue record for this title
is available from the British Library

Stay safe online. Egmont is not responsible for content hosted by third parties.

FSC
www.fsc.org

MIX
Paper from
responsible sources
FSC® C018306

THE REALLY FRIGHTFUL NIGHT

Kristina Stephenson

EGMONT

Once upon a stormy night there was a tall, tall tower with a pointy roof, a creepy corridor and some rickety, rackety stairs.

At the top of the stairs a witch with a watch was dreaming a scheme, a *long green dragon* was lost in sleep, and a little Princess was snoring!

Lightning flashed.
Thunder roared.

And Sweetle Beetles niggled and **clacked** as . . .

. . . something went bump in the night!

Well, the witch went on dreaming,
the dragon stayed sleeping,

but the little Princess started . . .
. . . screaming!

"Someone has stolen my teddy!"

How fortunate then that
Sir Charlie Stinky Socks,
his fearless cat Envelope
and his good, grey mare
were *also* in the tower that night.

And how lucky that *they* woke up!

"Hurrah!" thought Sir Charlie.
"A Damsel in Distress."

And with one quick polish of his trusty sword
he set off to look for her bear.

Trip trap, trip trap,

into the **creepy corridor** he crept.

Sweetle Beetles niggled and **shoved**.
A Shadow crawled on the wall.
But *nothing* could stop the knight on his quest.

Well, *almost* nothing, that is.

For along the **creepy corridor** there also crept . . .

. . . a smell!

Uuuuurrrrghhhh!

Now, clever knights in tall, tall towers
know smells might lead
to something.

So wise Sir Charlie
covered his nose,
and canny Sir Charlie
followed it –

trip trap trip trap – to a little wooden door.

Under the door
the smell crept out and

creaaaaaak

a bold, brave knight crept in.

Over a pot of green bean soup
hung a gaggle of *Ghastly Ghouls*.
Dribbling, drooling,

guzzling,

gorging,

slurping,

burping

and . . .

WORSE!

Envelope gulped.

The *green* mare gagged.

Sir Charlie tried not to *giggle!*

Good old Sir Charlie Stinky Socks knew
what too many beans could do!

And with one quick flick
of his trusty sword . . .

. . . he opened up a window!
"Tis I, Sir Charlie Stinky Socks!
I need to search this dining hall."

And he tossed out the last of
the green bean soup
(and with it, the terrible smell.)

In the tall, tall tower
(with the pointy roof)
the *Ghoulies* weren't so *ghastly* now,
and outside the beans were
growing.

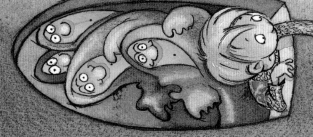

No, wait! That's a differe...

Back to the dining hall. Back to our hero –
who didn't find the bear.

But on that stormy night
at the top of the tower
he did hear some scary . . .

. . . clanking!

Was this the sound of
a thief on the run,
escaping with
the Princess's bear?

Only Sir Charlie Stinky Socks
would dare to find out.

Clickety clack,
clickety clack,

tippity,
tippity,
toe.

He ignored the Shadow
that lurked on the landing,
and the Sweetle Beetles
who watched him go . . .

. . . out to the rickety rackety stairs and . . .

That faithful cat Envelope took
no persuading.
Nor did the loyal grey mare.
They followed the lead of the Sweetle Beetles

and bolted down the stairs!

More's the pity for them. Indeed!
For, had they stopped,
had they waited
they might have heard
the wailing!

The wailing that came from below!

. . . out to *a clanking, headless Ghost!*

Now, sensible knights when they hear
scary noises never, ever run. **No, no!**

They stand their ground.

They think a bit.

And they *laugh* in
the face of danger. **Ha!**

Because patient Sir Charlie Stinky Socks
knew just what was going on.

If *most* of the Ghost was at the top of the stairs . . .
. . . then the rest had to be at the bottom!

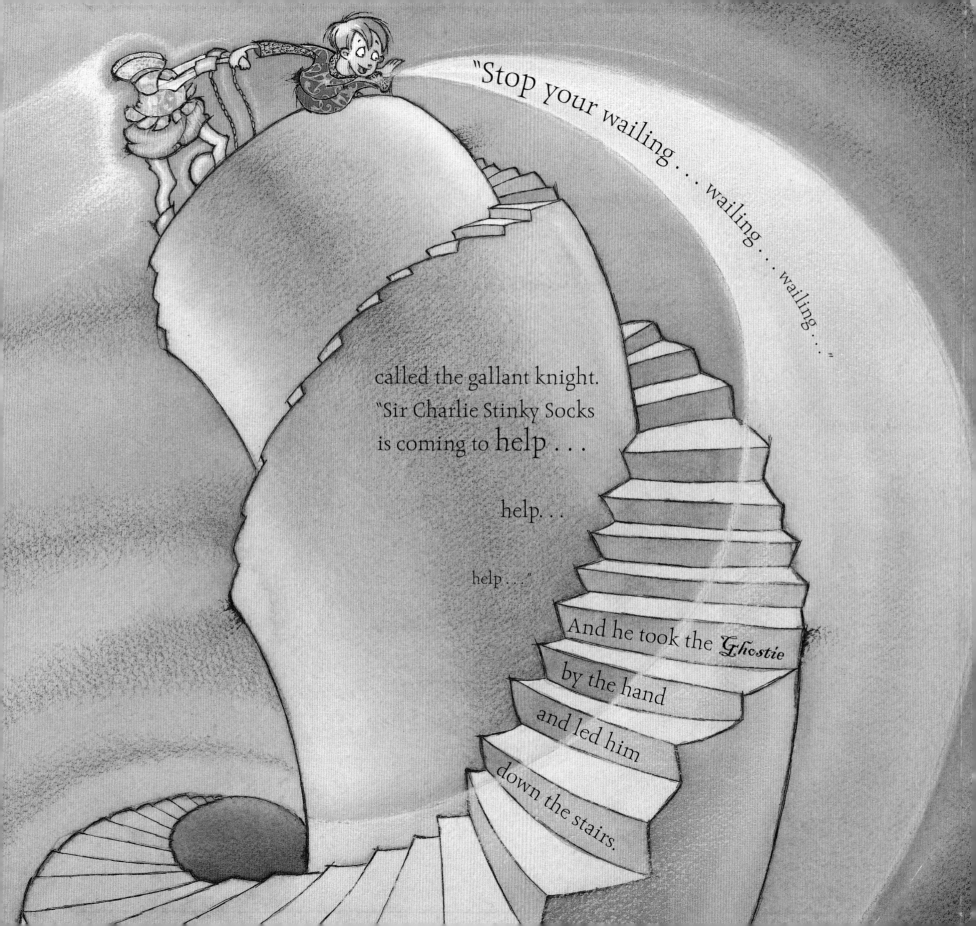

"Stop your wailing . . . wailing . . . wailing . . ."

called the gallant knight.
"Sir Charlie Stinky Socks
is coming to help . . .

help. . .

help . . ."

And he took the *Ghostie*
by the hand
and led him
down the stairs.

It was really rather dark at the bottom of the tower.
It was also completely empty – except for a truly
grateful head, and the cat and the good grey mare.
(Oh, and a somewhat sneaky Shadow
that followed them down the stairs.)

There were no Sweetle Beetles.
There was no missing teddy.
And there was nowhere left to go.

Oh woe!

Had Sir Charlie failed the Princess?
Was it time to hang up his sword?

Well, yes, once he'd spotted the mysterious lever
waiting for it on the wall!

Grrrrrrrrrrrrrrrrrrrrrrrrrrrrrrrrrrrrrr

CLUNK!

The lever shifted.

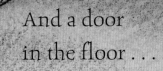

And a door
in the floor . . .

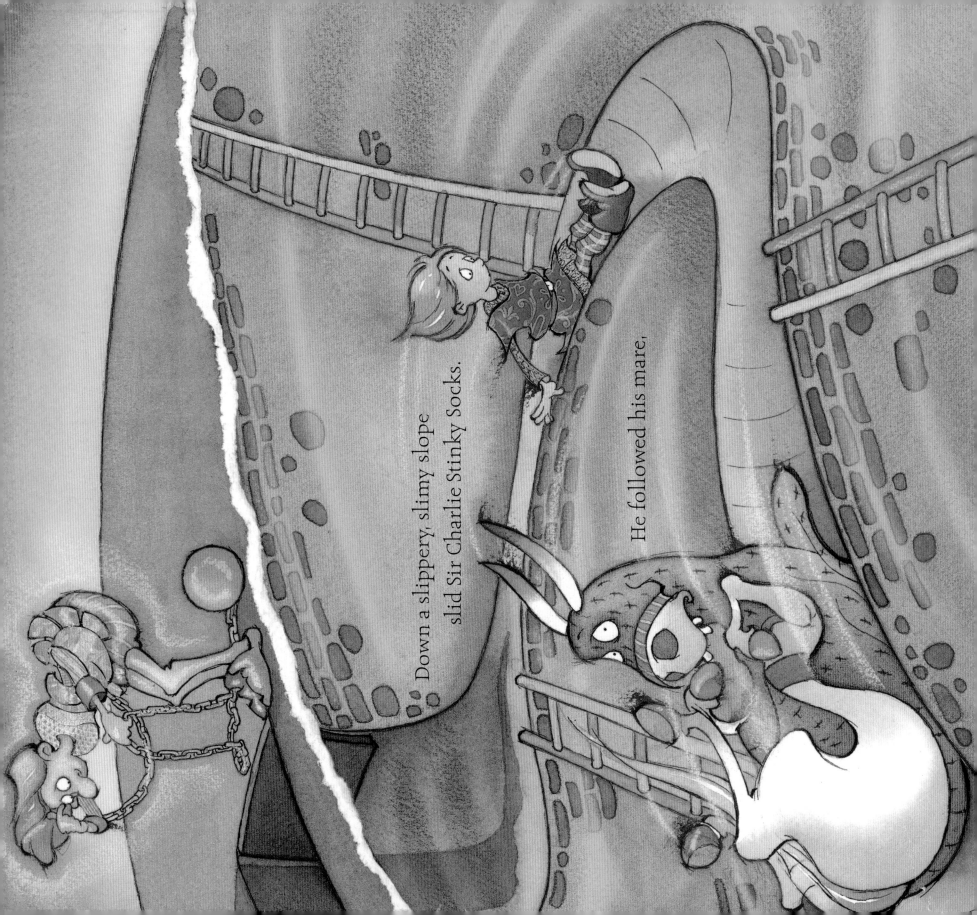

Down a slippery, slimy slope
slid Sir Charlie Stinky Socks.

He followed his mare,

his faithful cat and

a trail of Sweetle Beetles.

Down,
down,
downdiddy down,

right to the very bottom.

Where, quite without warning,

the Sweetle Beetles dropped . . .

. . . the Princess's bear!
Yes, there!
In a dark and dismal pit
at the feet of . . .

The **CELLAR DWELLER!**

Envelope froze.

The grey mare fainted.

But Sir Charlie didn't falter.

He may have forgotten his trusty sword

but he hadn't forgotten his courage.

"In the name of Sir Charlie Stinky Socks," said the bold, brave, curious knight, "tell me what's going on!"

Sir Charlie glared at the Cellar Dweller.

The Cellar Dweller looked . . .

. . . at the floor.

"Just as I thought!" said Sir Charlie to the monster.
" **YOU** made them steal the bear."

The monster shuffled.
The monster shifted.
The monster burst into tears.

"If *you* lived at the bottom of a slimy slope
where it's damp and dark and lonely
and if *you* didn't like the thunder and lightning,
I bet *you'd* do the same."

With that, the sneaky Shadow that had followed
them shuffled into the light.
Would you believe it,
attached to the end was
a smiling little Princess who looked at the monster,
looked at the cellar and
looked at the rubbish around.

"This is no place for a monster to live,"
she said to the Cellar Dweller.

"Perhaps she wouldn't," said kind Sir Charlie.
"Maybe she's not that bad."

"No, I wouldn't," said Sir Charlie.
"A *knight* would seek permission.
He'd climb to the top of the tall, tall tower
and ask the Princess himself."

"But wouldn't he be s . . . s . . . s . . . scared?"
stammered the Cellar Dweller.

"Of what?" said
Sir Charlie Stinky Socks.
"The *Ghoulies* aren't ghastly,
the *Ghosties* stopped clanking
and the only monster is . . .
you!"

"Oh no it's not,"
said the Cellar Dweller.

"Haven't you met the Princess?

She's spoilt, she's rotten,
she's always screaming
and someone like that
would say *no*!"

And all was well in the tall, tall tower.
Until the witch's watch struck two.

Then . . .
lightning flashed.
Thunder roared.
And *something* went

BUMP in the night!

"Pick up that bear and come with me.
I know somewhere much better."

This time the witch and the dragon woke up.
The witch didn't notice Sir Charlie Stinky Socks
sneaking out of the room. The dragon didn't spot
the cat and the mare tip-toeing through the door.
And neither of them spied the Cellar Dweller
sleeping soundly under the bed. Instead . . .

. . . all they saw was the Princess's teddy,
lying on the floor.

So the long green dragon
and the witch with the watch
tucked the teddy safely back in.

"Night, night, sleep tight.
Don't let the Sweetle Beetles bite."

And they didn't you know . . . .

. . . because on that frightful night
they had better things to do!

THE END